Grace and Glory

Grace

and

Glory

poetry by
Irma Frey Stevens

HALEY'S
Athol, Massachusetts

International Standard Book Number (ISBN): 1-884540-45-7

Haley's
Post Office Box 248
Athol, Massachusetts 01331
1.800.215.8805

Illustrations by Sergio Braz Caprini.
Cover photograph by Tammy (Tamra) Fleming Maus.
Book and cover design by Marcia Gagliardi.
Printed by the Highland Press.

Library of Congress Cataloging-in-Publication Data:
Stevens, Irma Frey, 1924-
Grace and glory : poetry / by Irma Frey Stevens.
p. cm.
ISBN 1-884540-045-7
1. Christian poetry, American. I. Title.
PS3569.T451553 G73 2000
811`.54 21--dc21

99-042543

For Tamra

Contents

Illustrations

The drawings listed above were done by Sergio Braz Caprini especially for *Grace and Glory*.

"From all that dwell below the skies, let the creator's praise arise . . ."

Isaac Watts

Grace and Glory

Morning mist married itself
  to the sky.
Maytime foliage formed a meshwork
  in shades of green.
Spring had unseeded itself from winter,
while people mingled and buried
  themselves in necessities.
Their singular faces flashed expectancy
  or were dormantly dull.

Planned plantings awaited germination,
then portions of grace for
  certain survival
and, finally, rainbows of glory
  with no endings.

Yearnings of a Soul

two forewords to *Grace and Glory*

Irma Stevens' poems reveal the yearnings of a soul that sees beyond the average mind. Such yearnings move the reader to wonder why one hasn't "seen" or experienced the same thing. One wants to take time to "look within and around" and ask, "What have I overlooked in my soul, my world, my friends?" Fragility, sensitivity, insight, yearning, awe, and pain are just some of the feelings that leap from the page and into the heart, awaiting response. Here is a collection of writings to calm the soul and lift the spirit.

Rev. Jeanette Burton,
retired Methodist minister

Grace and Glory is a true treasure of the poet's heart and spirit. She has a wealth of ideas, depth of meaning, eloquence of expression, and a certain elegant style. What is most evident, however, is the feeling of her soul.

To some readers, a few of Irma Stevens' poems become an expression of the Self. Through them, they may find a place to feel close to the Whole, close to home—an incarnated place of transcendent relation.

Regina Renn,
Jungian analyst

Stirred by the Sound of Church Bells

an introduction to *Grace and Glory*

I was born in the 1920s in a borough of New York where no tree grows—Brooklyn. I played in a small concrete back yard. It had an iron fence around it. Maybe my love for rhythm and melody was first stirred by the sound of church bells outside, the hymn-singing in the great European-style cathedral (part of the building that was my birthplace), or the piano music frequently played in our "parlor." I think my appreciation of sound and beauty was enhanced by our move to a small town, Clinton, in central Massachusetts. There, I was greeted each morning by bird songs. There, too, I first experienced the enjoyment of wide open areas of rolling hills. I came to love trees, especially, and the lush greens of summer after woodlands had "breathed so long through snow." When the sun came out after ice storms in New England, I saw diamonds. "You bless me with your radiance," I wrote to winter trees. I also felt gratitude for sea breezes and delighted in the family's summers at cottages in Newburyport and Salisbury. Some poems were written during a sojourn at the ocean. Inspiration also came during visits to Lake Sunapee and living for a while near Bristol, New Hampshire.

I was always a lover of flowers and derived pleasure from the colors and beauty of gardens, from small plots to the grand Botanics I saw when visiting England. The travel bug continually bit, and it took only a few occasions—visits to Niagara

Falls and the Grand Canyon—to result in poetic expression. I am very conscious of creation being of divine origin, a gift for all who have attempted to praise it in words, hoping to be a voice for other nature lovers.

From a very early age, writers significant to me were hymnists: John Wesley, Fannie Crosby, Martin Luther. As a young child, I memorized all stanzas of the great Lutheran hymn, "A Mighty Fortress."

I was also influenced by the Quaker poet John Greenleaf Whittier, by the transcendentalist Ralph Waldo Emerson, by Emily Dickinson, and more recently, by May Sarton. When I became a student of foreign languages, I was strongly drawn to Hermann Hesse and Rainer Maria Rilke in German, to Paul Claudel and Paul Valéry in French. I believe I was attracted to these writers because of innate, spiritual tendencies as well as to elements of lyricism and music in language.

Music has always been a major joy in my life. I chose not to study piano, as was expected of girls in many families during the era of my upbringing. My request for drum lessons was turned down—boys only! I liked the mellow tone of the marimba and was thrilled by hearing on the radio the great vibraphone playing of Lionel Hampton. At twelve, I was given a marimba, had six months of lessons, continued self-teaching, and, as an adult, played on stage as well as in local nursing homes and churches.

New interests began to appeal to me, and as my percussionist activities faded, so did the structure and rhyming of my poetry. Writing changed to freer style. Was it the "tra-la, tra-lee" rhythmic beat of my early years evolving into the more somber and steady pace of maturity?

I have immensely enjoyed children, their sparkle and genuine sincerity, their coming to us "trailing clouds of glory." When the youngest of my own three children was about ten, I left full-time housewife duties on the home front for a short-term morning position at a Yeshiva, a small Orthodox Jewish Academy. There, I had the pleasure of introducing middle school pupils to poetry, preparing a poetry recital for them at a closing ceremony, and receiving acclaim from a young rabbi. Very recently, I shared my poetry with more mature students, "children of all nations," in the English as a Second Language program at Clark University. I was convinced of poetry's universal appeal.

I have been inspired to write poetry, above all other reasons, because of human love and friendship. I have experienced the ecstasy of togetherness and sharing, the anguish of partings, the emptiness of loss. Poems were born of my deep sensitivity to the natural beauty of people and empathy with their hurts and sorrows. Hopefully, the poetic message will cause an in-common recognition that may help to lift "the essence-hiding veil."

I am of that generation and part of society where repression rather than free emotional expression was expected. Tears, particularly, remained in the heart. So, some of my poetry has a sad quality. I think many readers will understand.

Grace and Glory belongs to my devoted friend Tammy (Tamra) Fleming Maus who conceived the idea of collecting my lifetime-poems into a book. Tirelessly, she prepared them for publication and, with loving determination, nourished, encouraged, and inspired my ever-wavering creative spirit.

My sincere appreciation is also given to a few special people who, throughout the years of our growing, gave me "the courage to be" and who recognized in my poetry a voice worthy of being shared: Maurice White, D. H. Wolf, Mary Rist, the Ortwin Renn family, and Pauline Harpin.

I am grateful for the helpful suggestions and skillful editorial work of Marcia Gagliardi; also, for the inspiration received from my children, grandchildren, friends, and for the blessed memory and hope-giving of the late Lloyd R. Stevens and Dr. Maybel Bruce.

My main acknowledgment is of the Creator who graces us all with glorious seasons of life!

In conclusion, through poems of happiness and pain, I hope others will see nature's wonders more vividly, enjoy children truly, and love earnestly.

I know that my Redeemer lives. More than all else, I would like the readers of my poetry to know that comfort.

"And heaven and nature sing . . ."

Isaac Watts

from *Joy to the World*

Lifelong Worship

In springtime
when all is new and budding,
hidden pulses are beating,
young and weak things stirring
to be born into earth's living.
In pastel tints of springtime
we worship you!

In summer
when all is full and flowing,
the lately grown invigored,
joy mingles with the straining
to reach the goal envisioned.
In vibrant greens of summer
we worship you!

In autumn
when glory precedes fading,
and rising blends with falling,
aware of no undoing,
the matured are bravely serving.
In golden tones of autumn
we worship you!

In winter
when stillness is as dying,
the triumph of a ceasing
suppresses active being.
Beautified, age lies waiting.
In winter's quiet whiteness
we worship you!

Too Beautiful for Words

Creation's God is waiting to be praised,
to be honored with the gift of words.
   What words suffice for this?

And yet there is . . .
sunshine's warming power,
water to refresh,
sea-swept air for breath,
the earth producing nourishment
or awaiting seeds
to supply replenishment
   when hunger comes.

To respond to creation
for its gracious share . . .
   What words suffice for this?

Seaside Sunset

Traffic moved over the bridge.
A siren distantly wailed.
Seagulls screeched along the shore.
Motorboats whirred loudly.
An airplane's engines droned in the sky.

Children on the darkening beach
shouted responses to parents'
   sharp calls.
The waves continued their
   ceaseless thunder-hushes,
and the sunset—silently, beautifully,
   peacefully—
         said good night to the day.

Evening Flight Out of Boston

In awe the tiny human eye
directs its glance through a clear
plastic-covered oval just two hands high
and sees, framed by a massive silver
manufactured wing,
green marshlands along the bay
where sea gulls dip and soar.
A single sailboat adds serenity
as the city skyline disappears.

After the plane's earth-departing roar,
the sun puts on a setting performance,
revealing a golden-orange lake.
Next, a deep pink streak
sinks into a purple cloud-blanket
as beautiful as a child safely sleeping.
Cerise to fuchsia borders an arc,
blushing blues.

This vivid panorama,
multi-thousand miles above an ocean,
suspends the airborne being
in eons of delight!

On the Marginal Way

Kissed by the sea breeze
on this day of grace
I rest
on a gray cliff
high above the shoreline.
I receive nature's beauty
and allow the surf's sounds
to mute life's hurting voices.

Refreshed, I descend
to walk with others,
grateful again for humanity.
Real chords of consciousness
form a vital melody,
a song of oneness for many
on the Marginal Way.

Like Snow Geese in Flight

We spread our fragile human wings,
ascend to heights in clear-blue skies,
transcending clouds and cumbrous things.
We touch another traveler on the way,
viewing, singly, a distant scene,
dark-edged, hoping for purity,
empowered to fly into endless day!

The Winner Is . . .

We earthlings have our music.
Our human dance interprets joy,
while in the arc above us,
staccatoed scales and avian chords,
and movements borne
by windswept grace
vie for creation's grand awards.

Perennial Contrast

In the city, she loosens the soil
of her meager plot,
prepares a small place
for seedlings--it's spring.
She provides water and tenderly cares
for the flowers that beautify
the days of her summer.
She waits as the autumn and winter pass
until the joy of her planting reappears!
The cycle reveals,
though her presence is gone,
a little loveliness year after year.

While in the wilderness
strong, ancient greens
nourished by nature,
protect creatures, innocent, rare,
until maneuvered machines
swiftly remove what gallantly grew,
leaving acres of emptiness,
seasons of loss.

My Nature's Disaster

Why could I not stop
the saw's shrieking so cruel,
the wounding, the felling,
the planet's small loss?
My sin of omission :
  Not saving a tree.

Its presence remains for me
there in blue space.
Each season recalls to me
its freshness renewed.
Its height hovers over me
invisible now.
Its protection is lost to me,
its shadow, my need.

Solitary Strength

Through glass I see
  the solitary tree
quiet, strong, standing
  on its one leg—
  its trunk solid on snow—
rooted to earth, unable to let go
of unseen myriad attachments
  hidden, feeding far below.

It does not need a human touch,
but reaches limbs toward
  the omnipresent sky,
receives with gratitude
  wind, rain, sun,
unasked for gifts of grace.
It hears no word of love,
  no caring murmurs,
yet listens to the sounds
  of the universe :
creaturely cries and nature's
  mystical notes.

How similar are we—
I, solitary as the tree
stand silently—one limb this winter
  having no surface hold,
a being, rooted, nourished
  invisibly,
holding on to deepest bonds,
thankfully taking in
  freely given favors
  of earth and air,

tuning in to visiting voices,
alert to woodland melodies
and noises of the busy world.

Through glass I see
  the solitary tree:
Thriving! Also like me—
without human touch
or whispered words of love.

Return from Arizona

Red rock is nowhere.
The scene is green.
The dusky Navajo shows no wares.
Faces are much paler here
and lighter the sky-blue above.

Lilacs in bloom scent the air.
Apple trees blossom white
while desert flowers settle in stone.
The size of falcon, hawk, and quail
is reduced in the black-capped chickadee.
But balsams, maples, and red oaks stand
taller than the mesas' pinyon pines.

And all the deepness that remains
—like the song—
"is in the canyons of my mind,"
fathoming the various ways
of earthly sojourners, east and west,
people who come and ever go,
as warm and cold seasons come
  and ever go.

March

The March morning, cold and colorless,
   entered day,
shroud-like and still—no creature stirred
the frozen ground. Waters iced.
Brittle branches wore winter black and grey.

I questioned : Why so long this season's
waiting time?
Pleading followed : Grant life again.
Then, imperceptibly, there came a movement
slight,
changing from wafting into wind—
a stirring by a force invisible,
enlivening by an unseen power.

Warmth did not return
to thaw the hardened sod,
nor was dullness made more bright.

I know the answer now :
A March day may seem like a thousand years,
but the wind blows where it will
to resurrect the dead,
to cause renewal,
and *when* . . . .

To Trees, Ice-Covered In Early March, 1995

From your domain of cold air
  and clouded sky,
clothed in silver grey, you bow down to me.
Your bare arms, no longer dark but crystal clear,
bend low, some fingering the ermine blanket
protecting your hidden source.
Others, with teardrop pearls on every twig,
extend widely on contra sides
as if to embrace the flesh-bound creature,
  small below.

The sun punctures itself into day,
and your ice-coverings are transformed
into stunning diamonds.
Admiring, I look up into your sparkling face:
You bless me with your radiance!

Spring-Sweet Air

The spring-sweet air
and green renewed
encourage, urge hope
  to revive.
Dying dreams take lighter form.
Night bows out to
  favor morn.
Doors are opened,
once closed by cold.
A season reenters
with warmth and song.
We continue on
  life's circling roads
  leading to
  a centered goal.

April

So long the woodland breathed through snow.
No creature stirred its silent depths.
The fact that life lay there below
would seem but one of nature's myths.

Then April, with a magic hand,
awakened all beneath the sod,
in beauty clothed a barren land,
revealed again the power of God!

Little Flower Bed

Lying there in place all day
semi-circling around the yew, called "Peter's tree",
two clusters of pale pink impatience, at right and left,
having heart-shaped petals
and tiny center spots of deeper shade,
cuddle together close to the earth,
but tilt slightly skyward
while a row of crimson relatives
positions brightly in between.
A few velvet soft purple petunias nestle among them.
All affirm togetherness in beauty,
appreciating meager sunshine.
A stray day lily, a guard in orange dress,
stations itself above the others,
each morning featuring uncurlings
that form trumpet openings
exposing to light pollen-holding stamens.

When evening comes,
there is a quiet folding, blanket-like.
Then nighttime's angel arrives to watch over
the little flower bed.

Early September

I cared for them all summer long,
watering to prevent thirst,
heading marigolds and petunias
  to assure renewal,
turning hanging fuchsia for
  equality of sun,
and weeding all for surface breath.
I gave them devoted, daily attention.
They blossomed proudly in
  color-competition.
And the birds wanted for nothing here.
I filled feeders with sunflower seeds
  by the millions,
satisfied blue jays and others,
like the flashy cardinal and its dullish mate.
They arrived at an appointed time each day
to feast; while mourning doves
ground-fed contentedly.
Petite, black-capped chickadees
and raspberry-red finches
shared the ever-full cylinder of thistle.
I chased the cat to assure their safety,
so the winged ones flourished—
  having a bountiful summer.
How great was our separation
in that September's celebration!
My constant caring knew nothing
  mutual:
Flowers bloomed.
Birds sang.
I got along.

End of Summer Gratitude

The "white singing moment of peace"
comes in the sun's warmth
when the leaves are still
or in the cool of evening
before the August moon
silvers the waving willows.
Needs are supplied,
the answer to simple prayer.

Return in October

Fuchsia sunset reflected,
and water shimmered bright.
Then one star appeared in the
autumn sky.
We were silenced by the sight.

My gratitude soaked into the quiet.
The goodness of having you there
sponged out every tear of loneliness
because beauty was ours
to share.

Foliage glittered golden
in the final rays of day,
and those moments would gild
my memory
when you needed—again—to
go away.

Again

Refound ! A golden road—
at dusk, when lavender tinting
bathed the horizon,
and a crescent moon,
a bright silver fingernail,
stenciled the sky.

To return here alone
aching with longing,
an icicle
piercing waning summer,
is a futile retrieval
of another autumn.
But changing seasons,
shadows of winter,
do not preclude another return,
the refinding of a golden road
—and love.

Late Autumn

Small grey creature on a grey tree limb,
with tiny paws meeting across your front
like a narrow belt on a white apron,
your black and nut-shaped eyes meet mine.
Why do you stop to stare
when winds give hints of winter's touch
and you must gather sustenance
to store in hollowed hideaways?
   Why this time-out gaze at me?

Warm behind the frosted pane,
I feel the momentary fright our eyes betray,
not knowing what cold days may bring
before the thaw, the hope of spring.
Fear unites us, bush-tailed dweller
of the woods.
But not for long . . .
Our brief eye contact ends
with your fleeting leap to other limbs.
Your furred form is gone.
Squirrel-small and needing sustenance,
a being made rigid by winter's touch,
I stare into empty space,
   daring no leap to other limbs.

Winter Breakfast

On this cold morning,
every rooftop matches others
in white sameness.
Some lawns, invaded by plows,
are marshmallow masses,
others, peaceful pure plateaus.
My breakfast is an egg.

A hungry bird flits by the window pane,
casts no bead-eyed glance kitchenward.
It disdains to consider my protein source,
but parks its minute form at the feeder,
pauses, and then partakes
of small-sized nourishment.

I recall summer's sunflowers,
towering, facing skyward.
They seem complete, their centers
forming definite circles.
Their destined height achieved,
they have triumphed into wholeness,
and are ready to yield seeds,
a winter food-choice for some.

Watching the bird-feeder at breakfast-time,
a simple pastime, a possible summation:
So much might be derived from
the least of these—
an egg, a bird,
a flower, a seed,
this little thought of mine.

Lookout

I must look out at the snow again.
It blankets this quiet night
and hides the spring as the coming years
keep hidden from my sight
what may become mine—or what may not.
Whose footsteps will print a pathway
to my wintering heart's closed door
to harden over or softly change
patterns of snowstorms before?

The window is frosting over.
I turn away from the outdoor view
to interior white-walled space,
surrender myself to the season,
to the action of everyday living
in my appointed, unshadowed place.
Here winter allows no regression
and spring's potential invites
an outward look again.

Winter Tree and Me

God gives much grace
to the winter tree,
the bare-branched, weakened winter tree.
It stands sustained despite the storms.
It breathes through ice and
buffets wind.
Least loved, it silently awaits
the warmth of spring when it may burst
the buds it holds invisible
through all the cold and sunless hours.
Potential glory, long unseen,
is harbored by this unwatched tree.

I, too, stand weakened by the storms,
breathing through ice—indifference,
buffeting wind, person blown,
patiently waiting to release
the love within, the warmth so deep
it stays sustained through sunless hours.
And much is harbored within me
to whom God gives his care and grace,
just as it is given to the winter tree.

Mere Touches

Patches of white nestled
in the small hollows
of the old oak's arms.
Outlines of white softness edged each
ancient limb.
Around the strong trunk
a white scarf wrapped wide.

Below frozen ground,
feeding, strengthening,
unseen vital roots
permit victorious continuing life.

Mere touches of age defy.
They simply outline.
Hidden warmth and food
nourish endless springtimes.

Seasons

Summer's verdant background
graces the feverish earth
where low-lying red impatiens
and bright yellow chrysanthemums
add dazzle to fertile gardens
displaying multi-shades.

Too soon, blossoms will blacken,
hurt by a sudden frost,
like a window-shade closing out warm
sunlight.
But sumac will wave crimson fans,
maples dress in gold,
and leaves, blown about by autumn winds,
pretend to be orange flames.

Then the icy breath of winter
silvers bodies of water
and whitens the frozen land.
Peace and quiet will testify
to a cycle of seasons subdued.

Summer's child grows into adulthood.
Life's vibrant prime disappears.
The winter of old age signifies
—a cycle of seasons subdued.

". . . with a child's glad heart of love . . ."

J. E. Leeson

Inheritance

Life's tapestry cannot be raveled,
so interwoven are its strands.
It grows in beauty as time passes.
Patterns are formed by children's hands.

The threads of love, however weakened,
from birth remain, mothers keeping
children sustained by silent joining,
present in joy and in weeping.

Gifts of Love

Knowing what great things
can be done,
some mothers magnify their hope.
They bring to being, in pain and joy,
a child . . . and say:
Hold out your small hand.
Reach for a star.
Dare your own moon walk.
The planet is yours.
Receive it!
Add your little light.
Share gifts of Love.

Song at Birth

Once upon a summertime,
a tiny baby came,
"trailing clouds of glory,"
knowing not her name,
nor how to speak
nor what to hear
in this world's symphony
full of notes unsounded
in her still, small realm
of infancy.

Child Actress

As the butterfly spreads its lovely wings
delighting those who see,
so the child may choose the stage
to enjoy fantastic flight
in scenes of make-believe.

Butterfly wings gently close.
The child from the spotlight retreats.
But the curtain remains up,
and a sequenced act begins,
casting a matured heroine
into a living reality.

Parent and Child . . .
Running Toward Each Other Along the Shore

Tides of time
hold waves of joy
and harbor secrets
like the sea,
all ours to take at
crest or ebb.
While parent, child,
who race along
the sands of time
throughout life's tide,
sing silent alternating pleas:
come to me
run from me
meet me
surpass me
return to me
run *with* me
pass me by
never.

Echo of Poet Whittier

Blessings on my little man!
Shod in white with suit of tan,
dimpled babe who all too soon
will hearken to a whistling tune.

Then in sneakers, jeans of blue,
lured to boyland's rendezvous,
far from me he'll roaming go
in fields and woods, where rivers flow.

Joy be his along the way!
Sunlight shine on him each day!
Loving heart, one wish restrain:
To join him—whistling a refrain.

Son Gone

They ask me how you are,
you in your faraway place
where I have never been.
I answer, "Fine. He's doing well,"
knowing no truth, of course . . .
you never write or call.
They do not ask me how I am,
here in this familiar place without you.
I wonder just how "fine" *I'll* be
when you, at long last, return.

To a Youth Condemned

I would not listen to them
when they called you
what you are—or seemed to be.
I knew the truth of your reality,
your perfect being
before it was scarred
by some like those who spoke.

The evidence was there, they proved.
Yes, I saw it.
but I saw more
(because I love you!)
And wish I could have made them
see more, too.

Knowing and feeling the whole of you,
both sides—within, without,
I shall hold high before you
the vision of the inner only,
that you may rise above
what you seem to have become,
and be again your true, unhurt, unique
and holy self.

A White Boy Speaks . . .

My dad grew up in a country town
where he never saw anyone brown,
or yellow,
or any color but white.

Steve's dad always lived on a city street
where everyone he happened to meet
had dark skin like his.
It seemed all right.

But Steve and I are glad to be
where there are some people like him
and some like me.

We can't believe
it'd be fun to get grown,
just seeing skin like one's own,
and knowing there could never be
such fine twosomes as Steve and me!

Hampton Beach with Andrew

Noise, confusion, traffic.
We were bus passengers,
bound for the beach.
We merged with crowds on the boardwalk,
strolled among them on the shore,
bobbed in well-populated waves.
Later, we feasted on fast foods
and challenged games of chance.

A day's consumption of summertime
to honor an annual promise
made to a young grandson,
to experience his joy
and love's power to share
another's wish fulfilled.

About Laura, Age 6

Little Laura loved me.
It was just for a day.
She seemed to be so lonely
when I met her on my way.

So, I walked beside her.
It could not be for long.
We shared the woodland's treasures,
and I listened to her song.

Then the whir of wings and wheels,
signaled that we had to part,
but little Laura's loving me
remains a note to cheer my heart.

Snow Day with Grandma

Little figure in the snow,
silhouetted like the trees,
don't you mind the bitter breeze?
"Watch me, watch me—how I go!"

Sleds and saucers, boots and caps
mingle in the drifts of white.
Laughing child, are you all right?
"Did you see my flip-flop flops?"

All the sunny afternoon . . .
up the hill and down again.
It's getting dark. Once more, then—
"Zoomin' down I saw the moon!"

Home and food and bathtub rite,
chatter, action like a clown.
PJ'd figure, quiet down.
"Must I go to bed tonight?"

After a Grandson's Visit

There is a mother-love
after the mothering,
after the nurturing,
after the wedding.
    It is a more detached adoring,
    greater gratitude for a rarer presence,
    and sweet freedom from
    discipline-duty.

No wonder that after his
    welcomed visits
or overnight stays
(when the parents retreat),
his good-bye depletes my
    life of sparkle,
that light in boy-blue eyes.
My empty hand still needs his touch.
I miss his laughter's music.
Most of all, my cold heart wants
the special holy warming
of his very wonderful love-response
as if *I* were the lowly Christ-child
—and *he* presenting the gift of a Magi!

Amanda's Tree

A tiny pine
began to grow
in Auburn many years ago.

Each day,
more beautiful and tall,
it spreads green branches
over all,
makes music when
   the wind goes by
and often seems to
   kiss the sky.

Joy is mine
since it came to be
I call it
   "our Amanda's tree"!

Thoughts on Being

A grain of wheat—
to grow or die.
A bird-song,
music for the sky.

Snow blanket—
changing soon to green.
The miracles
of nature's scene.

A little girl—
a woman born,
as hope-filled
as each new, pink morn.

A mother's life—
ever-giving,
the essence of
continued living!

Upon Seeing Children at a Statue of Mary and the Christ Child

The growing green,
the distant scene,
children dimly view.
They sit content at
  mother's side.
They stand in peace
  on surface soil,
unaware that another child
once graced their common earth
—knew protection, too—
grew and gave in purity,
sacrificed totally,
then powerfully came,
quiet as a statue
  in a silent wood,
to dwell in all who truly know
the God who loves
  little children so.

". . . for the joy of human love."

F. S. Pierpont

Caprini

Loving You . . . In All Seasons

Thinking of you
in springtime
is being restless as buds
ready to burst into bloom.
Thinking of you
in summer
is being refreshed, as if by
surf-spray at the seashore.
Thinking of you
in autumn
is being awed as by crimson-gold
horizons.
Thinking of you
in winter
is being warmed as at a fireside
during a snowstorm.

Being with you in springtime
is having beauty—
better than blossoms!
Being with you in summer
is feeling vitality—
stronger than breakers!

Being with you in autumn
is knowing brightness—
grander than red leaves!
Being with you in winter
is peace—
pure and silent as snow in the forest.

Life's Mystery

Love is life's great mystery,
to those who find it, a sweet treasure,
a mutual fruitful discovery,
precious times of sharing pleasure.
So real is love's fragility,
so temporary is its joy,
to preserve it everlastingly
and let no fate its charm destroy
is a universal mute desire,
a hope that defies the futility
of that mingled peace and passion-fire:
Love—life's great mystery.

True Love

Know my being, know me really!
Love my littleness unique.
Lift the essence-hiding veil.
Find the genuine you seek.

I appreciate *your* person,
unsure self, so very dear.
Strive no more to prove your power.
I can love the lack you fear.

How at peace could be our living,
if in mutual recognition,
each saw the other's sad unwholeness,
and cherished it into fused fruition!

Yearning

To see the gap, the deep abyss
between what should be and what is,
can cause despair so very deep.
Desire comes for dark, for sleep,
unless the hope is present still,
to find a unique place to fill,
a little link of love to be—
someone's bridge to eternity.

Space Together

The small star seemed so close
  to the moon that night,
the sky-space between them
  might have been hand-spanned,
but reality, of course, denied such nearness.
The single truth is—
  a *place* was shared.
A heavenly residence held the
  small star, the moon,
  offering permanent room.

Your brightness is as far from me
  as the moon this night,
  but beaming in the distance
  there is a truth :
My small star and your grand light
reside in an eternal sharing place.

Distant Presence

Thoughts merging across an ocean,
mutuality of caring hearts,
  like waves resounding,
eyes meeting in dark and daylit spaces,
the touch of same spirits both waiting
  for glory.

Why such anguished unity
when absence separates?

Unconditionality

I do not hear my pulses beat
and yet I breathe, I live.
I can not melt a hardened heart,
but each day, I forgive.

I can not hear the raindrops
staining the window pane,
but there is a song within me
which no storm will restrain.

What power out of silence
and non-visualized great grace
sustain a love eternally,
heal deepest wounds, all wrongs efface!

Life Boatsong

Two can make it.
One can, too,
single file or two by two.
Life is but a passing dream,
we the boats upon a stream.
Double oars some have to row.
Others solo-paddling go.

Winds and currents, gentle be,
waft and ripple merrily.
Balance boats to prove it true :
One can make it.
Two can, too.

". . . in days of calm, in hours of strife."

L. D. Reed

Advent Calendar

"Try to remember"
each day in December.
Though many doors close,
windows still open wide
to give entrance to sunbeams
brightened by lovelight
dwelling in heart frames
shining through shadows
as days go by.

New Year

All forward is the heart's direction.
A faith-filled born-anewness
clings to every ray of sunrise,
lends bravery to just being,
gladdens days with gratefulness.
The shattered self pretends
a wholeness veritably returned,
and hope obliterates the shadow side.

All forward is the key sustaining.
For if one backward glance is dared,
a single thought turned to yesterdays,
former anguish reasserts,
the mind is trapped by tangled threads,
the body, straining toward
tomorrow,
is changed
to
pillared
salt.

Interior Particles

New fallen snow has purity,
unsullied whiteness, virgin clean,
and so remains until warm sun
melts the covering of the green.
Then turf, an earthiness, appears
with dark and light vitality.

Inside, in newly furnished houses,
wooden objects, solid and strong,
receive upon each hard surface
particles that do not belong.
They disturb until they disappear
to reveal an unwilled polish.

Lost in time are the angel-robed.
Seeds will replenish, years include
peelings of alternating shade
and dazzling holy interludes.
Mature domiciles then become
sincerely speckless, softened, probed.

Choice at Daybreak

What shall I choose to listen to first:
the news of the day?
the birds in the sky?

At the flick of a finger, the world would
come close
through the wonder of radio waves.
But with no other device,
just a listening ear,
no birds would come near, so far
is their sky-realm from mine.

In living, there really is no choice at all.
I am part of the happenings,
broadcast or not,
to support or prevent or ignore.
The bird song is distant, its meaning
unclear.
Any responding is needless for me.

So, I wonder what will matter most
on the unchosen day that I die.
What will mingle with my ghost:
the news of the day?
the birds in the sky?

Wild Soul

The wild soul never dies.
The sludge in the river
impedes flowing,
and inspired thought
defies concentration.
To organize is as futile
as aligning falling
autumn leaves.
But incubation is open-ended.
The creative impulse anticipates.
There is birthing ahead!
New life within settles,
surges, somersaults.
Water lilies surface.
The humming of springtime
will not be silenced.
The wild soul never dies.

Does Time Heal?

The healer came and closed the wounds.
The injured one entered life again,
weakened by loss of sacrificial blood.
All who encountered saw scars
and heard suffering cry out from the past.
They knew : time had more healing work to do.

Illusion

The jogger follows his planned path
his muscles toned,
a picture of physicality in prime,
his mind diet-conscious,
his passion : bodybuilding health.

The sitter, in a wheelchair every day,
some limbs atrophied,
is an image of power passed,
his mental vitality unseen :
a life-thirsty, idea-abundant mind.

Which would attract a wholeness seeker
or one dissuaded from boredom's pit?
Who is most well, more tending to share,
to strengthen another's integrity?

The jogger's heels disappear,
dust in the wake.
The sitter remains,
an oasis of possible healing.

Returned from Pain

Oh! wordless joy of being with you again,
returned to being
freed from pain
which, when it held me in its grip,
took self away, and self away
from you, whose goodness near
I could not feel.
Your warm touch upon me
did not, could not, cause to cease
the pain that swept me into nothingness,
into an empty realm far from all
the living world.

But now I am back,
free and fearless,
not bound by remembering how it was,
nor able to surmise how it might recur.
I only know the wonder
of being myself again
—with you.

Come, stay near me now.
Let us share this gift of gladness.
The very air is buoyant breath!

Eggs and Words

Do you know how incredible
the simple egg is?
Its outer part so fragile,
a quite thin shell
that holds within such wonder,
as our body, the thin-skinned covering
all may see
hides the self's strong verity.

The egg's inner substance
is a colorless fluid protecting a yellow sphere—
the yoke—centered,
receptive, nourishing.

Do you know how much a word
is like an egg?
Its little visible look and modest sound
hardly reveal the meaning,
the soul within ;
somehow there is a guarding
from what is lying deep,
like dreams, if unretrieved
from silent sleep.

Will you dare to crack the shell
of my words' true content
and fathom more—a life-giving nugget—
a golden, grand birthing,
a mercurial winging into regions above
when I deliver *to you* this ovation :
I love . . .?

Simple Truths

What is—is.

To be is to be.
Now is forever.
Love can be never.
People come and go.
God stays.
Green returns.
Sun fades.
Sky remains.
Words erase.

To Keep the Flame

What does it take to capture earth's beauty,
to sustain the glory of seeing the wonderful:
  a painting?
  a photograph?
  a poem?
God bless the creators who capture creation.
Safeguard them!
They are fragmented, fragile, finite.
Without them there is reliance
only on dreams and memory—
also fragmented, fragile, finite.

". . . and grace will lead me home."
J. Newton

Caprini

Home Ownership

This fragile earth is pieced with land,
cubes, squares, encirclings
of multi-shaped buildings,
places called home, owned
for a while,
numbered and claimed by one,
who proudly whispers:
"This is my place. *I* own . . . !"

An entrance possessed,
a door, personal key-controlled,
enable clear knowing
of power to earn.
There is a conscious reward:
being a grateful caretaker
of a chosen tiny fraction
of this most vast and fragile earth.

From a Rooftop in South Boston

Pastels and grays
and dark red brick,
tree greens,
water colors,
bay windows,
chimneys, stalwart sentinels
against New England cold,
distant blue hills . . .
such simplicity and nonchalance!

In contrast, across the way
is the Kennedy Center . . .
imposing, white and grand.
It attracts people from all nations.
The ambiance of prominence
and social concern
reminds of things presidential.

From a rooftop,
Boston's great little people,
always on the edge
of the harbor's uncertain currents,
stolidly stare at the
famous family's memorial.

Our Belonging Place

The "windows of the world"
are there for all.
We see a TV scene of
   myriad streets, countries, waterways,
and watch how life goes on
beyond our sphere.

But how comforting
   attachment is
to a small space that we own!
Though darkness frames
   our beings,
light greets us everyday
through special squares
   of sun or clouds,
very particular views
granted only at *our*
   belonging place.

Old House

Here in this high-ceilinged place
in empty space, memories float
more numerous than doorways.

Secrets of generations
drift from narrow closets.
Past families enjoy or weep.

The old oak looks through the pane
noting the people here today
unwarmed by furnace coal.

Their heating is automatic.
Windows are double-paned.
Food is microwaved.

Their talking comes through wires.
Buttons, switches regulate time,
but their insulation fails.

Better Mansions

Better mansions must be built
completely strong, no missing parts,
to meet the purpose of each place,
the reason for being in the spaces of time.
Nearing the finish, that final touch
is marred when any portion lost
cannot be found or brought to light.
So, a shadow rests on the edifice,
not to remain rejected, unknown,
but recognized for its hidden power,
a hardening stone to kindly own,
to uncover from darkness and
resultantly cause
a perfected structure, well-rounded
and sure
with a final corner squared at last,
the foundation secured.

". . . where cross the crowded ways of life."

F. M. North

Caprini

Busyness

The active world,
the churning days
patterned with people
around us swirled.
Busyness . . .
kept us in separate places,
yet, we were near
when you were here.

Now the outer movement
conceals the inner storm,
prevents the quiet tear.
Doing-time prevails.
Each day my swallowing schedule
allows no time to deeply care
that you are there.

Not the Luckiest

People who need
go about seeking
something to do,
something to read,
something to look at,
someone to listen,
because they are missing
  people they need.

Restoration

Where paths converge
how great the gain,
the dual experience of scenic sights
and mutually known delights!

The same road trod
together paced
doubles notes of happy song,
enhances right, assuages wrong.

When paths divide,
just one alone
sees robins flock on springtime snow,
or sunrise color morning's glow.
The other views
no bird at all,
and the horizon's breaking day
is painted in drab shades of gray.

Then each must find
a singular depth,
create what only one may cause
a waiting world to wonder, pause:
An insight shown,
its seedling start
can root and lean into the light
emerge from black, to display white.

Then union is again restored.
Matured companions, joined anew,
challenge the future: Be and do!

Personal Choice

You said, "My preference was to be with you."
And yet, you did not come.
I wondered why.
These thoughts broke through:
How strange—we often don't do as we wish.
Instead, we do the not preferred,
perhaps because a stronger force
secretly thwarts our deep desires.
And what we wanted might not have served
to smooth our troubled way.
With this, we rest content
until the choice to meet again is made
and glorifies a day.

Constancy

Your Spirit-given wisdom,
your kindness on my way,
the bond in Christ
  between us
made years seem
  like one day.

Our purged and separate
  sorrows,
our lowly, yielded wills
all mingled to provide
what gracious Peace instills.

To Darn or Discard?

No one darns today.
Young mothers, and theirs, have
  freed themselves
of baskets of footwear with imperfections
  begging attention.
Women have no time for
  damaged goods.
It is easier to discard
  and buy anew.
Multi-stores have varieties of fabrics,
  price selections, too.

But now, alone with your one sock,
I dare to darn again—to mend
  two small holes, side by side,
  in the toe.
The needle pricks and slides across
  one gap—and back again.
Suddenly a heart is shaped
  by the tearing, joining of
  the two empty places.

So, the needle must repair
  the fragile cloth
with a denser network of stitches,
more repeated piercings—in, out, across.

Oh, flimsy hearts,
can any mending cure
  your threadbare beings,
restore the separated damaged areas

each stabbed by hurt, like steel,
now needing meshed parallels,
a crossing of intervals between,
a shaping into sturdy love?

Temptation whispers : discard-time,
a tenuous wish to abandon
favors the new out there
   in the gaudy market places
   of fabricated choices.
There is a needing to cover extremities
   and empty spaces.
Is anyone ever ready to pay
the stinging price?

"Lead, kindly Light . . ."

J. H. Newman

Caprini

Cosmic Current

We each see a different horizon.
On opposite shores some stand.
The incoming tides, like footprints,
leave varied patterns on the sand.
Bravely we scan the ocean
wondering which wave might be
the carrier of some treasure
to set our spirits free
and wash away the boundaries
that separate sea and sky
to permit horizontal footholds
while we blend into one region on high.

Prayer

May you know God walks beside you,
on the left or on the right,
and always goes before you
leading you in paths of Light.
Be assured God is behind you,
protecting, gently urging on,
and believe in One above you
in dark of night or brightest dawn.
Feel God's gracious presence in you,
giving Peace, Power, Charity,
including your special being
in creation's universality.

Waiting

Waiting—all creation is—
to be delivered.

Yet everyone is in a frenzy:
Producing—replenishing the earth,
duplicating kinds—turning out objects,
making sounds—or things to see.
So, new beings are formed.
Populations add numbers.
Fabricated products abound.
Synthesized notes and flashed pictures
fill the present!
While very few are from themselves delivered:
From fragments,
dimming veils,
halved beings,
blurred visions,
disconnected heartbeats . . . .
Waiting—for the wholeness
no one realizes is lacking
unless, perhaps, in sleep
disturbed by dreams
of vainly searching for a missing peace.

The Holy Lost

Each day we are called
to the secular world.
Earning is our necessity.
Our spirit is stifled,
our essence denied,
our purpose lacking clarity.

We long to retreat
to a hallowed place
to find deeper nourishment here
and reply to those who seek us out,
"To this I am called, why do you fear . . .
that I may not return to crowded ways
where loveless throngs await my touch?
When grown in wisdom my time will come
to bring the salvation they need so much."

In the hidden child is the chance for rebirth
if we dare to return to the holy lost
to retrieve from the depths our vanities
and sacrifice them at greatest cost.

We continue outer activity
among those similarly bound
not leaving strongholds to be alone
where the source of helpful power is found.
Mature, unwise, our youth's wings closed,
we remain hungry among the unfed,
unaware, unwilling to follow the way
where the redeemer still leads
    and has so humbly led.

Rebirth

When I knew only childish things,
this is how it *seemed* to be:
  A baby in a manger lay.
  A man bled, dying on a cross.
Deep silence lingered at a tomb
where lilies grew in silent bloom.
  Unbroken clouds hung everywhere,
  as darkness set in all around.
  Always I was so alone.

When childish things were put away,
this is how it came to be:
  The manger held a gift divine.
  There was no form upon the cross.
The silence at the tomb became
a voice that spoke aloud—my name!
While everywhere, clouds opened wide,
as Light and Love shone all around.
  Never again was I alone.

Anointing

Astonishing—on the ground
   of this planet
sheltered like the soul of a crab
   from the needle hurt
   of its own vigorous pinching—
how one can be transformed
   by a magnificent spattering of Fire
and bear the stamp of a work of art,
clearer than a Kodak reproduction,
by daring a leap into faith,
fearful . . . as if it were
   a net of lace,
and be caught by God, the savior.

Knowing the Way

To walk by faith and not by sight,
to shun the wrong and choose the right,
to know God glorifies the way
of creatures he has made from clay.

Abiding Love

In part we know you, God, today
but in eternity, we hope to see you
as you are—the perfect deity.
Our friends, also, we somewhat know;
they share the voyage on life's sea,
but human bonds are incomplete
because we are not free.

Look down upon us, God of Love,
and teach us more today—
How would you have us help to guide
those friends of ours who stray?
We would not be the ones to cause
a needless tear to fall;
your sovereignty alone permits
what sorrows may befall.

We hear the answer in your Word.
It says, "Abide in me,
and let my words abide in you
for then you will be free."
In Christ each one a branch becomes,
united to the Vine,
its good fruit bearing separately
led by the will divine.

And when a branch is downward bent
by storms without, within,
abiding love supports until
it upward turns again.
May we obey your great command

while finding in you peace,
as we befriend with purer love,
may your joy in us increase.

Gratitude

I thank
autumn's Creator
for eyes to see—
   misty-gray skies and
            patches of blue,
   winding roads under archways
            of gold,
   all nature glorified:
   The best of earth's beauty
   revealed to me!

I thank
our Creator
for the stirring
in my soul—
   Love dissolving sadness,
   opening a pathway
            to joy,
   a blessing of bright
            renewal
   because of friendship
   given to me!

Legendary

We are nighttime figures.
Capped, furred, and swathed in legends,
we bring packaged gifts,
silent after-dark surprises
to sleeping children and the poor.
Yes, we give of our surplus bounty
or sacrifice at times.
We watch glad receivers in the
  morning light
but we keep ourselves hidden,
covered by careful non-expression
of heartfelt adoration and love
  grown invisible.

If only hearts would open wide,
out-pour the feelings centered there!
Then the need might be removed
to deliver only material goods
wrapped in red and green.

At Christmas

The coldhearted awakened at dawning,
released from willful flight,
wishing to return to a true way
of kindness, goodness, and right.
The strongest greeted the lowliest
in lovelock, like petals unfurled.
Everyone melted in oneness
in the warmth of a God-present world.

Faith

One star, one birth, one Holy Night
may lead humanity to Light,
but many walk in darkness still,
in bondage to an erring will.

This patient Christmas prayer is mine:
that *all* may know God's Love divine,
and from their waywardness depart
so Christ may live in every heart.

One star to make the darkness bright,
a world reborn—some Holy Night!

Epiphany

The first full moon
of the new year appears.
Icicles have an emerald sheen,
the snow, an azure glow.

An epiphany star, a guiding light,
entices sojourners to alter course.
They leave familiar pathways
to discover a place of humble birth
and yield former ways to begin anew.

A king would want it so!

Shortly after Someone Dies

All is done.
The Lord of Life has again proclaimed,
"It is finished."
It matters little now
what was said or unsaid,
to reason why,
or regret our futile plunges,
faith-propelled.
The mysterious finger has written.

We had hoped to be channels
to let God's healing come through us.
Now we feel enveloping silence . . .
speech ends—prayers, too, for a while.
It is too late to consider
Any untried possibilities.
We fear, most of all, the glimpse
that may reveal : Our being and doing
were irrelevant in the other's life
and death.

What matters now
is what will be said and done
by us, faith weakened
and vision dimmed,
who realize that without God
we can do nothing.
We are the willing instruments,
would-be healing helpers,
the yielded ones who do not see
and yet believe!

Sharing

God gave us eyes to see with,
gave us Spirit-wings,
opened our ears for hearing
and made us love all things.

So, with newly seeing eyes
and souls that soar,
with open ears for listening,
and hearts that all adore,
may we meet eyes veiled by darkness,
touch spirits bowing low
and hearts that hatred show.

Then, God's own great glory
can light another's day,
so the dying know reliving.
Let love change each human way!

For we would not alone see truth
nor wing a lonely flight,
and fail to share our vision
each vacant day and loveless night..

Just as They Are

Just as they are
we want to love them
although they hear no
   fervent calling
to a pathway leading home.
So, help us see in them
   an image,
the shadow of a dying form.

Just as they are
unwhole, uncaring,
may we love them for
   your sake
who came that they
   might be
perfected, changed by grace.

And when, at last,
we love them purely,
just as they are,
   just as they are,
comfort us in our awareness
that they—not knowing you—
can not love us,
   just as we are.

Calvary Prayer

O, Jesus, bring me
to your feet
that I may look up
and see
the sweet compassion
of your face
and believe you hear me
when I cry,
"Remember even me!"

Vespers

On Enders Island
worshippers walked
to the chapel,
the sunset a backdrop.
We two simply watched them.
Our open window welcomed
   the scent of lilacs.

We were all in Sunday dress.
Our bodies bathed together
   in fading sunlight
   and springtime's perfume.
But our thoughts
prevented blending
and caused separation
as certain as walls.
Still, we heard bells ringing!

Response

I longed to give the gift of words
to vibrate in others' solitude,
to stir a quiet mind
or touch an open heart.

Was there a receiver,
a ready listener
to take my verbal offering
and answer,
    "Yes! I, too, believe"?

About the Author

Irma Frey Stevens lives in Auburn, Massachusetts, and teaches English as a Second Language classes at Clark University in Worcester, Massachusetts. Her education includes a BA in foreign languages and an MA in Biblical studies.

She has three adult children and seven grandchildren. She enjoys the natural world, reading, music, and friendships. Her faith in God is abiding and transcendent.